Suman Crosses the Karnali River

A Geotechnical Engineering Story

Written by the Engineering is Elementary Team

Illustrated by Ross Sullivan-Wiley

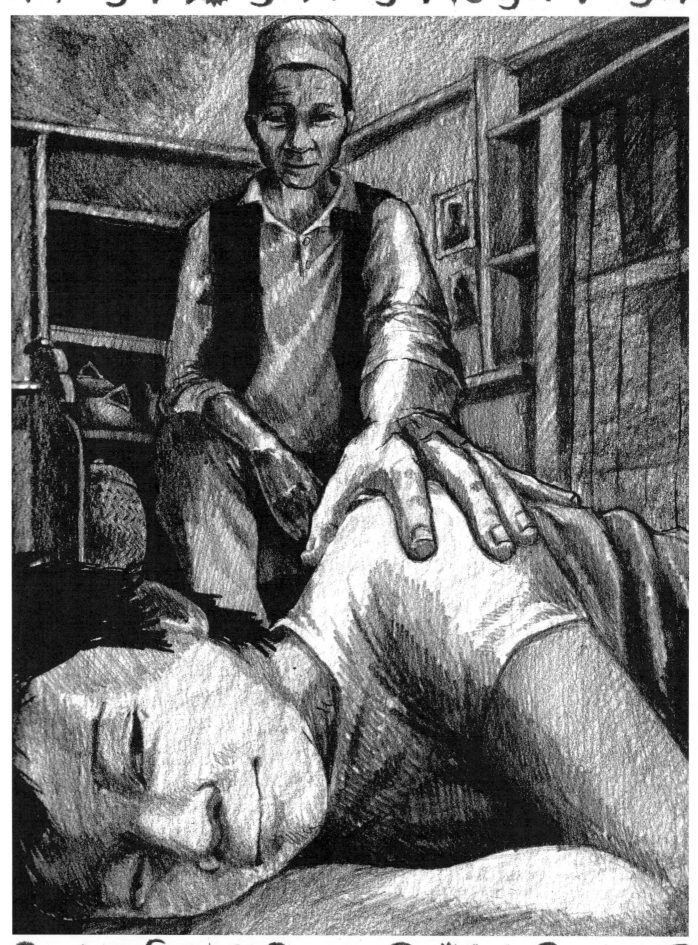

Chapter One	# Journey Through the Night

"Suman!" Buwa, my father, stirred me awake. "We need you." My eyes fluttered open. I lay there for a moment, not sure whether I had been dreaming. Through the window, the sky was dark—much darker than the misty blue I usually saw just before sunrise, when I normally awoke.

Buwa called me again. "Come quickly." A racking cough broke through the night air. It was Ajee—my grandmother.

My heart clenched as I sprang up from my sleeping mat and walked across the packed earth floor of the living room toward my grandmother. I could barely see Buwa's face in the darkness, but I heard the worry in his voice.

"Ajee needs to go to the clinic," Buwa said.

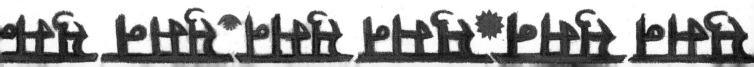

I helped lift Ajee out of bed and wrapped her arm around my shoulder. It seemed to weigh less than a bird's wing. We eased her to the door and guided her onto the cart we used for carrying vegetables from the field so she wouldn't waste energy walking. Buwa and I pulled the cart toward the Karnali River. Sunlight was just starting to shine on the golden goddess statue at the temple as we left the village, but by the time we reached the river, the morning light had turned the sky pale blue. Buwa lifted Ajee and helped her step across the sandbags laid in the river as a bridge. I followed behind them, carrying the cart.

Off in the distance, I saw the small stone building with a thatched roof—the medical clinic. When we arrived, Buwa told me to wait outside. I wanted to be with Ajee, but I knew better than to challenge Buwa, so I sat leaning against the building. I closed my eyes and, picturing the goddess statue across the river, asked for a blessing.

Chapter Two | A Distraction at School

The next day at school I kept staring out the window, thinking about Ajee. Buwa told me the doctor had given Ajee some medicine, and in a few days she would be fine. But Ajee seemed so frail. *What will happen if Ajee gets sick during the rainy season?* I thought.

During the rainy season, the rain often fell so hard that the river would flood and we couldn't go to school. If the floods were bad enough, we wouldn't be able to cross the river for anything—not even to reach the clinic.

"Let's go, Suman!" Dipesh said as he patted my shoulder, waking me from my thoughts. "We don't have much time before our math lesson!" I followed him outside. Dipesh and I gathered the flat rocks scattered around the

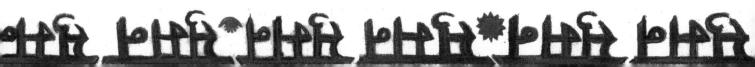

schoolyard from yesterday's game of ball and stacked them into a tower. Anna Miss, our teacher, jogged up behind us.

"Here we go again!" she said. "Are you going to be easier on me today? I'm a guest here, you know. Maybe you could let me win at least once!"

"We'll see," Dipesh said. "If you keep practicing, I think you'll be able to win some day." Anna Miss had only learned to play our favorite game a month ago. She said they didn't have this game in the United States, where she grew up. But as soon as she came to work in our school in Nepal, we taught her all the rules.

Everyone formed a line behind me. I picked up the

worn, brown leather ball at my feet and threw it toward the rock tower. The rocks clinked as they tumbled down. The next player—Anna Miss—grabbed the ball and tried to tag me with it before I could pile all the rocks back up.

I'd barely piled up half the rocks when the ball bounced off my arm. I was out of the game.

"Yay, Anna Miss!" my classmates called as they gathered around to congratulate her on her first win. Anna Miss smiled and thanked everyone, then crouched beside me to help pile the rocks again.

"Are you okay?" she asked. "I'm glad I finally won, but you never lose at ball." She turned her face and met my eyes.

"Besides, you seem a little sad today."

"I'm just tired," I said. Then I told Anna Miss about our nighttime journey over the river with Ajee.

Anna Miss nodded. "That sounds like a rough night. I'm glad your grandmother is going to be okay." She was quiet for a few moments. "I have an idea that might cheer you up a little," she said. Then she raised her voice so everyone could hear. "Despite today's win, I think I've proven I'm not the best ball player in the world. What if I show everyone a game that I grew up with—one that I'm good at?"

"That sounds like fun," I said, my spirits brightening.

"What's the game like?" Dipesh asked, coming up next to us.

"Just give me a few days to set it up. No hints before then," Anna Miss said.

Anna Miss began to usher us back inside for math class. I tried to think about her new game rather than how the river would change during the rainy season.

| Chapter Three | # A Special Project |

On the way home from school, my sister, Sita, and I passed the gold temple at the edge of our village. I looked up at the goddess carved into the pillar. She seemed to be staring down at me. I touched my forehead and asked for a blessing: that Ajee recover quickly.

Sita and I approached Shyam, a neighboring farmer. Every day on the way home from school, he called out to us, "Tell me, what did you learn in school today?" If he approved our answers, he would let us pass. If not, we had to tell him something else we studied. As we approached today, he was talking with another farmer. Pressing my hands together under my chin, I greeted them by saying, "*Namaste.*"

"Ah, Suman and Sita," Shyam said. "I have a different kind of question for you today—one that is not about school. Can you tell me what your *buwa* has to say about this possible project for our village?"

"What project?" I asked, wrinkling my brow and looking toward Sita. She shrugged, not knowing what Shyam meant either.

"He hasn't mentioned it to you?" Shyam asked. "If a respected man like your *buwa* isn't talking about this project, I wonder if we will go through with it." Buwa was one of the only men in the village who had gone to college. He'd traveled all the way to Kathmandu, the capital of Nepal, to attend. Sometimes he would tell Sita and me about the city and how Sagarmatha, or Mount Everest, towered above the buildings there. Now many of the other farmers come to him with questions about village politics. "Tell your *buwa* I will pay him a visit later this evening to hear his thoughts about this bridge project," Shyam said before turning back to the other farmer.

"Sita!" I said as we walked away. "Did you hear that? A bridge! Do you think it's true that the village is going to build a bridge?" Sita seemed to know how excited I was by the way she smiled at me.

"I don't know, Suman," she said. "You're the biggest gossip in the village, and if you don't know about the bridge, then there must not be anything to know," she joked.

I laughed. Sita was partially right. I liked to talk to all

our neighbors, and Buwa did talk with me about important happenings in the village. He always said it was good for me to understand these things, since I would be involved in village decision-making when I grew up.

As we got closer to home, I could see Buwa working in the rice fields behind our house. We live far away from Sagarmatha, in the Terai area of the country, where the land is flat and green. "Well, I guess I should go hear what Buwa has to say," I said to Sita. "What kind of village gossip would I be if I didn't know what was going on?" Sita grinned and headed into the house while I went to find Buwa.

"Suman! There you are," Buwa said as he saw me approaching. "I've been trying to finish turning this soil before dark. Now that you're here, you can take over for me so I can speak with your grandparents."

"Is Ajee worse?" I held my breath.

"Ajee is fine, Suman." I felt relieved, but wondered what Buwa wanted to discuss with my grandparents. "I need to talk to them about something else," Buwa continued, "something important for the village."

"I wanted to ask you about that, too," I said. "Shyam mentioned a bridge. What is happening?"

"Nothing yet. Just talk," Buwa said.

I opened my mouth to press further, but he raised his

hand, cutting off my question.

"I know you're curious, Suman," he said. "When we adults figure things out, I'll explain them to you." With that, he turned and strode toward the house.

Chapter Four | A Chance to Help

At our dinner of *daal bhaat tarkaari*—rice with lentils and curried vegetables—I listened carefully so I'd be sure to catch any mention of the bridge project.

"Suman, you are very quiet this evening," Ajee said. Her voice was still weak, but she sat straight and looked stronger.

Buwa chuckled. "He's waiting to hear the village news. Aren't you, Suman?" I gave him a big smile and waited for him to continue. "As you heard, the village is thinking of building a TarPul," Buwa said.

"What is that?" Sita asked.

"It's a special kind of bridge," Buwa said. "It is supposed to be good for crossing rivers during the rainy

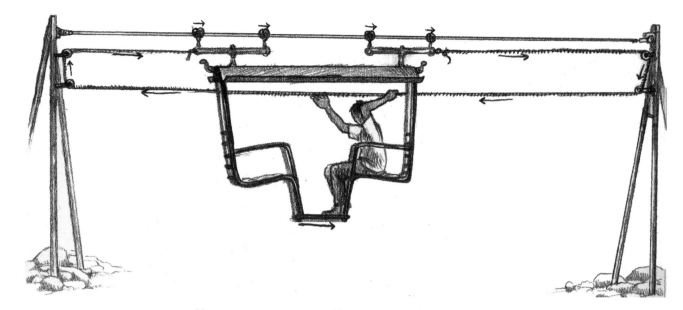

season. It allows you to pull yourself through the air in a small car hanging from cables above the water. I'm going to meet with the team in charge of the TarPul project tomorrow."

Everything was happening so fast! I could hardly believe Buwa's words. "Will it be done before the rains begin this year?" I asked.

"We hope so," Buwa said.

The sharp sound of Ajee's cough cut my excitement short. My grandfather, Ajaa, reached over to touch her shoulder, as if to give her strength. *This bridge is so important to our village,* I thought. "Buwa, do you think I could come with you to the meeting?" I asked.

"Yes, I think that would be a good idea, Suman," Buwa said. "You're getting old enough to help with a project like this. You may come with me."

Chapter Five | # Technology or Tradition?

For the second day in a row, Buwa and I rose early and walked to the edge of the river. This morning, however, my heart was light. From a distance I could see a small group of people pointing to various spots along the riverbank.

"Suman, this is Kedar. He is a geotechnical engineer. And this is David Mister," Buwa said when we arrived. "He invented the TarPul."

"*Namaskar*," I said as I bowed toward David Mister.

"*Namaskar*," David Mister responded. "I'm glad you've come, Suman," he continued. "It's good to have young people see how the TarPuls are built. Hopefully, by the time you're grown there will be many more technologies like the TarPul around."

"Excuse me, David Mister," I said. "What do you mean by technologies?"

"Well, a technology is any thing, system, or process that's designed to solve a problem. The TarPul is a technology that helps solve the problem of how to cross the river during the rainy season." He pointed across the river. "We'll anchor poles in foundations on opposite sides of the riverbank, then run two cables and a rope from the pole on one side to the pole on the other. The car that people ride in travels along the cables. The people riding in the car pull themselves along using the rope."

"I see," I said. I tried to imagine riding high above the river. What would it be like to look down and watch the water flowing past, knowing it wasn't a danger?

As David Mister and Buwa fell into deep conversation, I looked around. Kedar began to use a machine to push a long tube into the ground. Then he twisted and lifted it. As he laid the tube on the ground I could see dirt inside. I knelt beside Kedar to get a better look.

"This helps me to see the different layers of dirt in the ground here," he explained, as if he could tell I was curious. "It's called a core sample."

"Different layers of soil?" I asked.

"There are all different kinds of soil, rocks, and organic

materials that make up the ground," said Kedar. "As you go deeper, the mixtures change. Part of a geotechnical engineer's job is to figure out the makeup of the layers of the ground at a certain spot. Some types of soil are better for anchoring structures than others."

I looked at the tube and saw the layers inside. That I understood. But I still had a question. "What is a geo . . . geo . . . "

"A geotechnical engineer?" said Kedar. "Geotechnical engineers use what we know about science, math, and the layers of the earth to help people determine good locations for building structures. The TarPul that your village is going to build will be anchored by foundations on either side of the river. I'm here to help decide the best place to build the foundations."

"So you figure it out by looking at the type of soil?" I asked.

"Yes. I look at the soil and some other variables," Kedar explained. "The width of the river is important. If you put the TarPul at a wide point you'll need more materials and more support. We also look for areas that are unlikely to erode—where the soil won't be worn away."

"I know about erosion!" I said. "That's when earth or soil is washed away by water. It started to happen to the

terraces behind our house where we farm. Every time it rained, some of the soil washed away and the steps of the terraces wore down. Buwa and I built walls to support the terraces. They stopped the erosion."

"That's a good example," Kedar said. "Riverbends usually erode the fastest. The water washes away the soil on the riverbanks just as the rain washed away the soil of the terraces behind your house. We have to remember that when we're choosing a location for the TarPul. It wouldn't make sense to put the anchor poles and foundations where the riverbanks will erode quickly. I'm going to test the soil at a few other spots tomorrow, and then I can make a recommendation for where to put the TarPul anchors."

"I don't see why we need tests and recommendations." Buwa was standing near us. He crouched down. "The TarPul should be built where we always cross—at the narrowest point in the river. For thousands of years everyone in our village has crossed the river at that spot." He looked toward the sandbags where Sita and I crossed to get to school every day and where he and I had carried Ajee across the river. "Every time we have tried to build a bridge at any other point in the river, it has been washed away. Every time, we lose money and days of work. I am very grateful for this TarPul," Buwa continued, "but I see no reason why it should change the ways of our fathers' fathers." Buwa's voice had an edge of sternness in it. A hush fell over the group of men.

In that silent moment, Buwa stood and bowed towards the other men. Kedar stood, and he and Buwa bowed as well. I quickly did the same and scrambled to follow Buwa as he turned toward home. I didn't say a word, but my mind was whirling. Kedar's expression had changed quickly. A moment ago, he had seemed relaxed. Now, the look on his face reminded me of how I felt when I wanted to argue with Buwa about chores in the fields. There seemed to be trouble in the air.

Minutes passed as Buwa and I walked in silence.

"Buwa," I began, "When I was talking with Kedar, what he said made sense. It seems to me that putting the TarPul where Kedar suggests is—"

"Suman," Buwa said. "I know I said you were old enough to help with this project, but you are never old enough to disrespect your elders. You cannot challenge my decisions when you still have so much to learn about the traditions of our village."

Neither one of us spoke during the rest of the walk home.

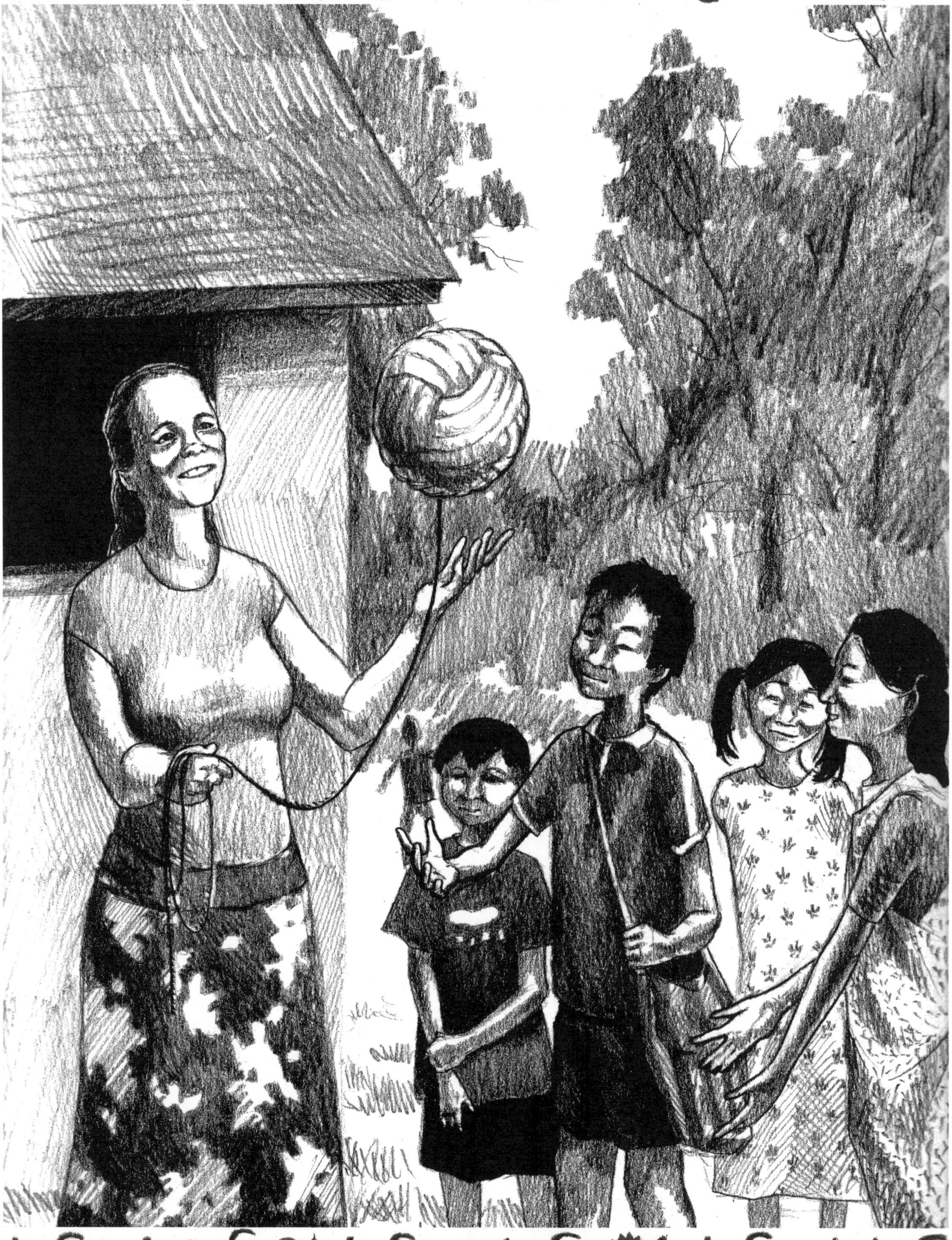

Chapter Six | # Anna Miss's Game

The next day, I stood alongside my school friends, waiting to see what Anna Miss had brought for us. "The game I'm going to show you," Anna Miss began, "is called tetherball. All you need is a pole, like that one," she said, pointing to a metal rod laying on its side at the edge of the schoolyard, "with a ball hanging from a string attached to the top of the pole."

"So what do you do with it?" I asked.

Anna Miss explained that two players stand opposite each other and try to hit the ball so that it wraps around the pole. "I know it sounds easy, but each player is also trying to block the other's try," she explained.

"I get it," I said. I ran over to the rod, picked it up, and

asked, "Where should I put it?"

"How about near the edge of the schoolyard, so we don't get in anyone's way?" Anna Miss suggested.

I pushed the pole into the ground. "Ready!" I said. We broke into teams and started to play. Dipesh stood on one side of the pole and I stood on the other. He hit the ball toward me, and I gave it a hard shove back. Instead of the ball flying back toward him, though, the pole fell over. It sloped down to the ground.

"Whoa there, Suman," said Anna Miss. "I think you put too much muscle into that swing!"

I ran over to the pole and pulled it out of the ground. Sand trickled down from the sides of the hole to fill the spot where the pole had been. I crouched to take a better look.

"We all know I'm the strongest kid in the village," I

joked, "but maybe this was just a bad spot for the pole." I thought for a few moments. "The soil here is sandy and soft, not firm. I wonder what would happen if we put the pole along the path from the school to the water well. The soil there is hard and packed down from everyone walking across it so much."

"That's a pretty smart idea," Anna Miss said. "Where did you come up with that?"

"I met someone yesterday. A geotechnical engineer," I said. "He was talking to Buwa about the best spot to build a bridge across the Karnali."

"Well, I think your idea is a good one," Anna Miss said. "We'll have to try it tomorrow, though. It's time for our math lessons. Everybody inside!" she called.

Chapter Seven | A Visit with Kedar

As I hopped from one sandbag to another in the Karnali on the way home from school, I scanned the riverbanks, looking for Kedar. In the distance I saw him writing on a notepad set on a large rock, like a makeshift desk.

"I'm going to talk to Kedar," I said to Sita. "I will be home in a few minutes."

Sita wrinkled her nose. "You're not the only one interested in the village's new project. I want to come, too."

"And you make fun of me for being nosy," I said. "All right, come on."

As we approached Kedar, I bowed in greeting and introduced Sita.

"*Namaste*," Kedar said. "What can I do for you?"

"Today at school I saw why the site where you build something is important," I said. I told Kedar and Sita the story about the tetherball pole and how tomorrow we would try to move the pole to firmer ground.

"That's very interesting, Suman," said Kedar. "It sounds like you've already started using a system that I often use to help me figure things out: the engineering design process. It's a series of steps that engineers use to solve problems. The first step is to ask questions—like your questions about where to put the pole and what the soil is like in your schoolyard."

"But how do you know if you asked the right questions?" Sita asked.

"That's where the next steps of the engineering design process come in. You imagine lots of different possibilities," Kedar said. "I'm working on that step now. I'm trying to imagine possible spots for the TarPul based on the information I've already gathered. Maybe you can help me." Kedar reached into a bag and pulled out a large map. He unrolled it onto the rock. Sita and I each held a side of the map and leaned in to get a closer look. "I've marked on the map all of the information I learned about the soil along the riverbank. Here is where people from your village normally cross," he explained, pointing to a line he'd drawn. "Over here is sandy soil. And there is firmer soil. Now, where do you think we should put the TarPul?"

"This spot would be closest to the medical clinic," Sita suggested, pointing to a bend in the river. "Maybe you should put it here."

"I'm not sure," I said. "At riverbends there is a lot of erosion." I smiled at Kedar as I repeated his words from yesterday. "I think I would put it here." I pointed to a straight part of the river with firm soil in the riverbanks.

"That's a good spot," Kedar said. "It's actually one of the spots I'm going to recommend to the village. Maybe you

two can stay around to help me with the next step: coming up with a plan to present to your father and the other men of the village. Then I'm going to create a small model of the TarPul site based on my plan. Create is the next step of the process. I can run some tests on my model, and finally move on to the last step—improve. I'll try to improve my site recommendation to make it the best it can be. You could try all of these steps with the pole for your game at school. I bet by the time you're done you'll have a sturdy pole in a good spot!"

I leaned back from the rock, resting on my heels and gathering my thoughts. "Kedar," I said, "the TarPul won't last if we build it where Buwa would like, will it?"

Kedar shook his head no.

"But his mind seems made up," I added.

Kedar nodded yes this time.

"Kedar? What if you can't change his mind?" I asked.

Kedar looked straight at me. "We can't move on with the project until I do."

"Or until someone else does," said Sita. We were quiet for a moment. "Suman, I think you should talk to Buwa."

"But I don't know if he'll listen to me," I said. "He wants to honor our traditions."

"I've seen this happen sometimes in other villages,"

Kedar said. "Your father is trying to balance many things—not just what the village needs and wants today, but also the decisions and wisdom of many ancestors. And he doesn't know me well yet—it takes time to build trust. If not this year, perhaps you'll have the TarPul next year."

Next year? I thought. *What if Ajee gets sick before then?*

....

At school the next day I took Kedar's suggestion and tried to use the engineering design process to find a good spot for the tetherball pole. Dipesh and Anna Miss asked many questions about what I'd learned from Kedar. Then we imagined possible locations. We used all of our geotechnical engineering knowledge to pick the site we thought was best. Then we played tetherball to test our site selection. After a few improvements, we found a great spot!

As I watched Dipesh and my classmates playing tetherball, the pole firmly rooted in the ground, I realized how important geotechnical engineering was to a project like the TarPul.

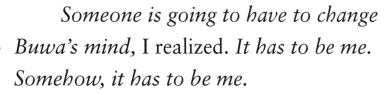

Someone is going to have to change Buwa's mind, I realized. *It has to be me. Somehow, it has to be me.*

Chapter
Eight

Facing Buwa

After school that day I stood with Buwa in the rice fields, helping him clear a patch of land. I listened to the rhythm of my shovel scooping the dirt and tried not to be nervous about what I was about to say.

"Buwa," I began, "I have been thinking about our conversation the other day by the river."

Buwa paused and looked toward me for a moment before asking, "What about it?" He went back to work.

I continued scooping dirt, looking down at my shovel as I spoke.

"I've been thinking about different types of soil and earth. The soil here is soft and good for farming. But it's not as firm and well-packed as the soil in the floor of our house.

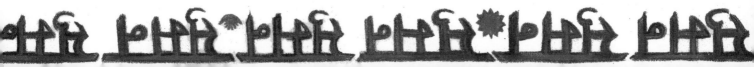

The poles of the TarPul need to be in firm soil so that they stay in place. Kedar told me that the soil near where we cross the Karnali is sandy. I'm afraid of what will happen if we build the TarPul there."

Buwa seemed to be listening, so I continued.

"I know that you are older and wiser than I am. You know much more about our village. And you've had more schooling. Some day, I hope that I will become as wise as you are. I need to be able to get to school across the Karnali even during the rainy season so I can learn as much as you did. More than that, I need to be able to learn from you and Ajee. We need the TarPul not just so I can go to school and learn from books, but also so we can keep Ajee healthy and strong. That way I can keep learning the traditions of our ancestors from her." I could no longer hear Buwa's shovel scooping, so I looked at him.

Buwa was looking in the direction of the temple.

"Suman," Buwa said. "Our country has gone through many changes. Not all of them have been good. People in this village trust me to use both my knowledge of the old ways and my education. They trust me to guide decisions." Buwa sighed. "Sometimes trust is a heavy thing to carry. I'm lucky that my son is becoming both educated and wise and can help me with that weight," he said. I breathed a sigh of relief that he was not upset with me. "I can see that you've truly thought about the TarPul and about the conversation we had. I think that you're right. It is my duty to make sure you and everyone else in the village will be able to cross the river, whether it is the rainy season or not. I will talk to Kedar tomorrow and ask for his recommendations about where to put the TarPul."

A huge smile spread across my face.

"I am very grateful to you, Buwa!" I said.

"Suman," Buwa said. "I am grateful to you."

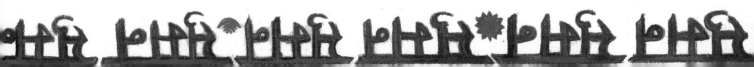
Chapter Nine | Crossing the Karnali

Two months later I sat with Sita, crossing the river in the TarPul. Being there made me think of Ajee. Once the TarPul was built, Ajee was able to visit the doctor more often. Now her eyes sparkled like they did when I was little.

From up in the TarPul I could see our village and the temple where I took my blessing on the way to and from school each day. On the other side of the river, I could see the medical clinic and our school, with farms reaching out for miles behind them.

I felt small in the TarPul, looking at the land below. But I knew in my heart I had been a part of something big— something that would be a blessing to our village for many years to come.

Try It!

Selecting a Site

If you lived in Suman's village, where would you suggest building the TarPul? The map to the right shows the Karnali River, Suman's village, and the medical clinic. Use the engineering design process to make predictions, test, and improve, just like Suman did!

Materials
- ☐ Soil
- ☐ Sand
- ☐ Gravel
- ☐ 2 pencils
- ☐ String
- ☐ Small paper cup
- ☐ Pennies
- ☐ Masking tape
- ☐ 6 plastic cups
- ☐ Aluminum pan

Analyze the Map
Should the TarPul be built close to the clinic or further away? Where does the river bend? How will that affect erosion?

Build a miniature TarPul using a paper cup suspended between two pencils, like in the picture shown above.

Test Different Types of Soil
Fill two plastic cups with soil, two with a mixture of sand and soil, and two with a mixture of gravel and soil. Make sure they are all filled to the same level. Try anchoring the pencils in different pairs of cups. Add pennies to the paper cup to see how well the pencils are anchored in each soil type. How many pennies can each type of soil support? What happens if you compact the soil with your hand? Or if you sink the pencils to different depths within the cups?

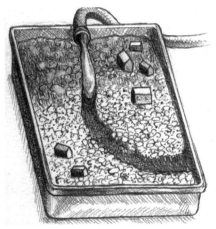

Choose Your Site and Test It!

Using what you learned by looking at the map and testing the soil, choose a site where you'd suggest anchoring the TarPul. Then test it out! Using the aluminum pan and the soil type you chose, create a model of the map shown above. Use a hose or jug of water to model the river. Add weights to the paper cup to model people sitting in the car. Does your TarPul remain standing?

Improve Your Selection

Use the engineering design process to improve your site selection. Are there ways you can make your model TarPul sturdier? Would different soil mixtures help? Would more compaction help? Do some more research to help make your TarPul site selection the best it can be.

Glossary

Ajaa: Nepalese word for grandfather. Prounounced *AH-jha*.

Ajee: Nepalese word for grandmother. Pronounced *AH-gee*.

Ball: A Nepalese game. After a player knocks down a small rock tower with a ball, he or she tries to rebuild the tower before being tagged with the ball by another player.

Buwa: Nepalese word for father. Pronounced *boo-WAH*.

Core sample: A cylinder of soil taken from the earth to show the layered structure of the soil below.

Daal bhaat tarkaari: A common Nepalese dish made with rice, lentils, and curried vegetables. Pronounced *doll BAHT tar-car-ee*.

Engineer: A person who uses his or her creativity and knowledge of mathematics and science to design things that solve problems.

Engineering design process: The steps that engineers use to design something to solve a problem.

Erosion: The process of soil or earth being worn away by water, wind, or ice.

Geotechnical engineer: Someone who uses what he or she knows about science, math, and the layers of the earth to help determine the best locations for building structures.

Namaste: An informal Nepalese greeting. Pronounced *nah-MAH-stay.*

Namaskar: A formal Nepalese greeting. Pronounced *nah-MAH-skar.*

Organic material: Any material that can be decomposed. It usually contains the remains of living organisms.

Sagarmatha: Nepalese name for Mount Everest, meaning "Goddess Mother of the World." Pronounced *sag-ahr-MAH-thah.*

TarPul: A type of bridge in which people sit in small cable cars suspended from steel cables that are anchored to posts built into foundations on either side of a river. Using a rope strung across the river, passengers are able to pull themselves over the water. The word TarPul means "wire bridge" in Nepalese.

Technology: Any thing, system, or process that people create and use to solve a problem.

Terrace farming: Planting crops in a series of steps or levels carved into a hillside.